Sasha & Sheila

ISBN: Softcover   978-1-9845-2666-3
        Hardcover   978-1-9845-2667-0
        EBook   978-1-9845-2665-6

Print information available on the last page

Rev. date: 03/05/2019

Additional copies are available at special quantity discounts for bulk purchases for sales promotions, premiums, fundraising, and educational use.

For more information, please contact:
Suzette Smith, 480.239.8561

Contact the author directly at **admin@ggferments.com**

To order additional copies of this book, contact:
Xlibris
1-888-795-4274
www.Xlibris.com
Orders@Xlibris.com

Our dedication to you

In honor of one of the most beautiful humans to ever walk the planet, my friend Sheila always had a smile to light up the world and a heart that only knew love

Sheila loved food and would feed anyone to cross her path. You were always welcome in her home, and everyone had a place in her heart.

Sheila lost her battle to lung cancer, and before she died, we created the story line for this series, and it is my promise to her that we change the way we look at food and create awareness of fermented foods and how foods can affect the health of your body. .

You are what you eat so choose your food wisely. Learn to grow food or find a farmer or farmers market close to you. Create a rainbow on your plate of fresh vegetables and love what you nourish your body with.

Sasha is a Southern girl from the country. She recently moved with her parents to the city.

Sasha was really sad to leave her red dirt, wooded trails and favorite animal friends behind.

She loved to go hang out with the pigs in the woods, keep company with the cows, hunt for chicken eggs in the coops, and ride the neighbors' horses. She worked hard in the garden, picking beans, pulling weeds, and carrying watermelons. It was her favorite time to be with her dad. Sometimes he even let her drive the big red tractor.

Sasha and her mom cooked the veggies from the garden. It was Sasha's job to cut the veggies for her mom to cook in the family cast-iron pan. This wasn't just any pan—it was *the* pan given to them by their grandmother, the same pan that was given to her when she started feeding her family. This was their most favorite pan to cook with, and it made everything taste a little bit better.

For special treats on a hot summer night, Sasha and her mom made fresh ice cream. Those were the best nights, chasing lightning bugs, swinging in the tire swing, and sharing ice cream with the neighbors. Everyone came together and brought a treat they made. The grown-ups would talk, while all the children in the neighborhood would play.

Now Sasha lives in the city. She is a little nervous because she doesn't know anyone in the city. She is excited because it is a new adventure for her and her family. So many thoughts and questions ran through Sasha's mind as they traveled to their new home.

Sasha thought, *Who will I play with? Where is the garden going to be? Are there lightning bugs to chase in the city? Where will we get our milk since we left Bessie in the country, along with all my animal friends? Who will feed the chickens and gather the eggs?*

Sasha and her family pulled up to their new house. It is very different. Her yard is small. Her house is smaller. Everything is smaller. At first, she was scared. Then she saw a girl about her age playing in the yard next door. She was about the same size as Sasha.

She smiled inside knowing she's going to have a new friend.

Sasha hopped out of the truck, and the other girl walked over and said, "Hi. My name is Sheila. Are you moving in?"

Sasha said, smiling, "Yes, we are. My name is Sasha."

Sheila helped Sasha as they moved in to their new home.

While they were in the kitchen, as Sasha's mom unpacked, Sasha found the family pan and pulled it out with pride. Sasha shared with Sheila that her mom cooked most of the family's meals in this pan. She told Sheila that it came from her great-grandmother.

Then she said proudly, "One day it would be *my* pan to cook for my family. It just makes our food taste better!"

Sheila looked at the pan. She looked at Sasha and asked if she could hold it.

"This looks just like the cast-iron skillet my mama has!" Sheila grinned.

They both laughed, and both knew they were going to be friends for a very long time.

Sasha and Sheila were always together. They sat next to each other on the bus. They both had the same teacher at school. And every day after school, they did their homework together in the afternoon before they went out to play together. When it was time to come in, they would take turns helping their moms cook the family supper. Sasha loved going over to Sheila's house to help cook because she always learned something new.

Sheila was fascinated with the foods at Sasha's house and how yummy they all tasted. She was starting to notice that her pants were getting a little loose. But how could that be with all the food they had been eating?

Sasha's favorite food was fermented veggies. She could sit down and eat a whole jar, but then they would be gone until she and her mom could make some more.

The first time Sasha shared them with Sheila, Sheila was a bit unsure. Sheila thought they smelled really weird when she opened the jar. But she trusted Sasha. She tried them, and to her delight, they were just as yummy as Sasha promised.

What was the magic about these veggies? Sheila asked Sasha, "What is so good about these veggies, and why do they taste so yummy?"

"Well," Sasha said, "these are fermented broccoli and cauliflower from our garden last year."

"Wait," said Sheila. "These are from your garden? From last year? How can that be? They are still crunchy! And what is *fer-ment-ed* broccoli and cauliflower? I don't even like broccoli and cauliflower, but I love these!"

"Veggies are still crunchy because they are fermented," Sasha explained. "Fermenting foods makes them last longer, and they are super good for you."

"How are they good for me?" asked Sheila.

Sasha smiled. She loved talking about her fermented foods because they were so much fun to make and fun to eat.

"Well," said Sasha, "long, long time ago, before people had refrigerators, they learned to ferment foods to preserve them. The fermented foods also helped their bodies from getting horrible diseases. Fermented foods help build our body's immune system.

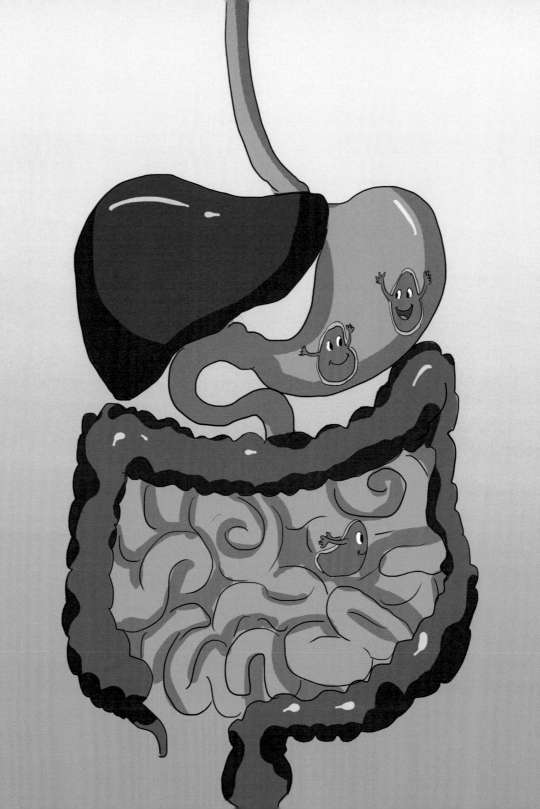

"You see, when you ferment foods, the food creates these great bacteria that get in your tummy and help your body grow in a good way. I like to call the bacteria *lacti bacti*. Lacti bacti makes it where I don't want to eat candies or cakes or drink sodas. Lacti bacti gives me energy and helps me sleep good at night."

Sheila thought for a moment. She realized she hadn't had any soda since she had started eating these veggies at Sasha's house. Come to think of it, she hadn't had any candy in a long time either, and she didn't even miss it.

Just last week, her friend at school offered her a doughnut, *her favorite*, and she took one bite and threw the rest away. It just didn't taste good anymore.

Hmmmmmm, Sheila thought, *maybe that's why my pants are getting loose.*

"Okay!" said Sheila, getting excited. "We have got to make some of these fermented veggies for *my* house."

Sheila looked at Sasha, the smile leaving her face.

"My mom is diabetic. She always craves sugar. Maybe these fermented veggies will help her not want sugar anymore!"

"Let's do it," said Sasha.

The girls got on their bikes and rode to the market. Sasha took Sheila to the organic section of the vegetables and fruits.

"We buy mostly organic veggies," Sasha said.

Sheila asked why "organic"?

"When some companies grow food, they may spray toxic chemicals on the food to keep the bugs off. This makes the food grow faster and bigger. But those chemicals get in our food. When we eat the food, the chemicals go into in our bodies.

"Yuck!" said Sheila.

Sasha nodded. "Right. We don't want that. That's why we buy mostly organic."

Sasha showed Sheila how to pick out vegetables. She showed her how she looked for broccoli that was nice and green and firm to the touch.

She then asked Sheila to pick out the cauliflower. Together, they grabbed some fresh dill, garlic cloves, and Himalayan salt and checked out.

When they got home, Sasha and Sheila washed the veggies. Then they cut the broccoli and cauliflower into bite-size pieces. Sasha got the filtered water and measured out the salt. She added the salt to the water and explained that it was the brine and that a 2% brine is great for most vegetable ferments. "We always use Himalayan pink salt" said Sasha.

Sheila finished her job and said, "What's next?"

Sasha grabbed some jars from the pantry. She showed Sheila how to stuff the jars with the veggies. First, they put the dill into the jar, then some broccoli, then some garlic, and then some cauliflower until the jar was almost full. Sasha carefully filled the jar with the brine she made, put one of her special glass weights on top, and then screwed on a lid with a funny looking plastic lid.

"What in the world is that?" asked Sheila.

This is a special lid that keeps the air out of the veggies while they ferment. When veggies ferment, they put out gasses. This lid allows the gases to escape without letting air in. Veggie ferments need an anaerobic environment to ferment properly. That means the jar needs to be air tight.

Sasha carefully placed the jar in the pantry. She told Sheila that they had to wait for five to 10, days depending on the temperature, then Sheila could take it home to eat.

Sheila was bursting with excitement to share these fermented veggies with her mom! After about a week, Sasha said they were perfect to put in the fridge. She took out the glass weight and put a new lid on the jar and gave it to Sheila.

"Here you go. Give this to your mom to eat a little bit every day."

Sheila did exactly that. Her mom was a little skeptical, mostly because of that smell. But when she tasted them, she thought the fermented veggies were delicious too! And just like Sheila, her sugar cravings went away. Soon the doctor lowered her diabetes medication. Sasha's mom told Sheila that if you eat the right foods, your body can heal itself.

Sheila just loved her new friend and all the fun things they were doing with food. She can't wait for their next adventure with fermented foods. Sasha and Sheila loves eating fermented veggies every day.

How to make fermented veggies

2-3 stalks of broccoli

1 head of cauliflower

3-5 clove of garlic

1 bunch of fresh dill

2% brine (73 grams of salt to 1 gallon filtered water)

Stuff jars with veggies, add brine with an inch to spare at the top.

Fill with water and add weight.   Screw on lid with air lock.

Set in dark cool pantry for 3-7 days, depending on the temperature.

Take out weight, add more brine if needed and close with secure lid.

Place in the refrigerator for up to a year and enjoy often.